林 鷺 著
Poems by Lin Lu

黃暖婷 譯
Translated by Faustina Nuanting Huang

生  滅
Life
and Death

林鷺漢英雙語詩集
Mandarin – English

台灣詩叢 • Taiwan Poetry Series 11

【總序】詩推台灣意象

叢書策劃／李魁賢

進入21世紀，台灣詩人更積極走向國際，個人竭盡所能，在詩人朋友熱烈參與支持下，策畫出席過印度、蒙古、古巴、智利、緬甸、孟加拉、馬其頓等國舉辦的國際詩歌節，並編輯《台灣心聲》等多種詩選在各國發行，使台灣詩人心聲透過作品傳佈國際間。接續而來的國際詩歌節邀請愈來愈多，已經有應接不暇的趨向。

多年來進行國際詩交流活動最困擾的問題，莫如臨時編輯帶往國外交流的選集，大都應急處理，不但時間緊迫，且選用作品難免會有不週。因此，興起策畫【台灣詩叢】雙語詩系的念頭。若台灣詩人平常就有雙語詩集出版，隨時可以應用，詩作交流與詩人交誼雙管齊下，更具實際成效，對台灣詩的國際交流活動，當更加順利。

以【台灣】為名，著眼點當然有鑑於台灣文學在國際間名目不彰，台灣詩人能夠有機會在國際努力開拓空間，非為個人建立知名度，而是為推展台灣意象的整體事功，期待開創台灣文學的長久景象，才能奠定寶貴的歷史意義，台灣文學終必在世界文壇上佔有地位。

實際經驗也明顯印證，台灣詩人參與國際詩交流活動，很受重視，帶出去的詩選集也深受歡迎，從近年外國詩人和出版社與本人合作編譯台灣詩選，甚至主動翻譯本人詩集在各國文學雜誌或詩刊發表，進而出版外譯詩集的情況，大為增多，即可充分證明。

　　承蒙秀威資訊科技公司一本支援詩集出版初衷，慨然接受【台灣詩叢】列入編輯計畫，對台灣詩的國際交流，提供推進力量，希望能有更多各種不同外語的雙語詩集出版，形成進軍國際的集結基地。

2017.02.15誌

CONTENTS

目次

生滅
Life And Death

春

從野地上的一朵小黃花啟程
糾結的冬風還不死心
緊緊追隨
我結霜的髮絲也還在意氣用事
臆測遠方的母親
再也沒有能力擁抱
最後的春

山

為何靠海這麼近
浪來浪去
浮浮沉沉
天晴還原本色
天陰一紙灰影
浪高浪低
進進退退
固執在沉靜的歲月

海

防風林外
白色波動的邊線
傳遞
家鄉逐日侵蝕的訊息

巨大的風車垂首悠閒
無風
只是望向冬陽下
一片永不蒼老的海

晨花

美的喜悅
被斜進的陽光照射
溫柔
釋放原始的野性
不思生
不思死
只是默默盛放

極冬

急凍的冬季
不停傳來死亡的消息
雪的原色失去純美
有些葉片
有些花瓣
凝結出血的顏色
紛紛飄下
無聲的嘆息

距離（一）

這麼近
又這麼遠
這麼清楚
又這麼模糊
我想放大心中的影像
縮小自己
重新躲回溫暖的子宮
漂浮
海的呼吸

禮物

醞釀了一生
我把最好的禮物
贈送給妳
不要妳的感謝
不要妳的讚美
只想妳好好握住
心中純良的玫瑰花
愛惜已經植下的芳香

鏽

時間窺視一個人
生鏽腐蝕

日日鏡中端詳自己
可曾仔細思慮
比以前更認識自己

那畏懼風寒的雙膝
開始擔心
能否支撐遙遠的過去

橋

夜色浸染窗外的風景
橋失去了身影
只剩下
一條流動兩岸的燈影

十字架

禱告沒有聲辭
雪白的流蘇開在牆外
盛讚季節

亮潔的白貝手珠
有母親初產的祝福

仰頭稱頌
巨大的十字天窗
無邪的光
正透視著四月的劇痛

肋骨

狠狠被拔掉一根肋骨
於是　這個人
有了一個
必須緩慢復原的空虛

他不知道那根肋骨
究竟失落在
狼還是人的嘴裡
只能暗自慶幸
流過血的身體裡面
還有一線生機

思念

母親的臉
存放在
我的思念裡
母親的聲音與形影
卻一再被拒絕在
每個暗夜
熟睡後
我最想進駐的
電影院

觀瀑

一種狂暴的美
以極度落差
傾瀉
現實與虛幻的視線
來不及思考
生死的源流與去向
陽光
寒顫地解說自然律

故人

說：生成台灣人
　　死做台灣鬼
說：活成苦命將軍
　　離不開
　　拼搏的戰場
今日有風又有雨
您是率真的自己
祭拜也成過去
目睹您巨大的身影
濃縮在
小小的骨灰甕裡

芝櫻傳奇

人走了
愛情沒走
他把妻子的話語
種成美麗
覆蓋的思念
蔓延整片綠色的長坡
開成一朵朵
胭脂色的小花
緊緊簇擁
傳奇

藤瀑

流洩
流洩
流洩白
流洩黃
流洩紫
流洩黑
老藤不老
催生不死的春天

回音

想知道
卻沒有回音
想回家
卻不敢說出家的位置
門如果開了
你一眼看到的會是誰
或者僅僅是
一切
已經不存在的
人間背棄

魚的想像

我不是魚
但我的出生脫離不了
一片廣闊無法探索的海域
海風的味道
經常喚醒我所嚮往的
自由呼吸
或許我曾經是一條魚
因為曾經被吞噬過
所以力求
一條魚該有的優游

質疑

雲淡風不輕
關於
一朵玫瑰的來處
突然從遠距離
開啟爭執
黃色的花瓣
堅持拒絕承認
來自不真實的
出生地
詩人信仰上帝
為何不質疑
背棄神的帝國

老

站不起來的日子
嗚咽
時間如果還堪倒轉
多麼願意回收
初生時
長命百歲的祝福
拿最後的
一口氣
來交換氣虛的無奈

紅樓詩情

被雨輕輕淋溼的淡水
享受詩人溫柔的擁抱
美麗的語言迴旋紅樓長廊
句句從不同國界的心靈
發出讚嘆

疤

不再無瑕
一失足
閃電
斜斜劈向
飽滿的
天庭

既然找不到
上帝的立可白
只好選擇
坦然
閱讀狐疑的眼神

客家藍布衫

山藍染布的藍布衫
裁剪客家婦女的冷靜務實
滾上幾道
不流於單調的襟上斜花邊
叮囑
已婚婦女簡樸唯美
讓未婚女孩加上些許花俏
好為她們呼喚
可能到來的春天

一座山

夠高了吧
身為一座山
視界已經毫無遮攔
只有陽光可以讓你明亮
雲霧不必你的應許
也會過來圍繞
做為一座山
大家都想知道
面對自己
你究竟怎樣思考

賣花女

望著來來往往的街道
繁華與熱鬧
是否距離妳寂寥的心
很遙遠
妳的花只開樸素的色彩
妳坐著的紙箱
能否支撐
生活給你的所有重量

如果（一）

如果
有一種美
與你匆匆相遇
或
僅僅
相互擦身而過
何妨讓游移的眼睛
喀嚓攝入
裝飾記憶的
風景

紅葉

一樹濃密
桃紅的葉子
逃離了
色彩的野豔
那
輕如羽毛的溫柔
又何必
被強求收斂

都市鐵窗

隔而不絕
陌生也可以留存
某種自然親切的日常
讓彼此的距離
成為視覺自然的透視
不淪落為
相互冒犯的魯莽

紅與藍

無邪的紅葉
在湛藍的天空
寫下
無比深情的
詩句

眼睛

有一種明亮
如燈
會在暗夜的林木
成雙發亮

請千萬熄滅
喜好窺視的慾望
讓自由與信任
不須慌亂地逃跑

你的畫

——寫給一位台灣畫家

你的山
有我們成長的仰望
你的海
拍打我們母胎就有的聲浪
你的船
負載一整座島
在太平洋上的重量

吊橋

搖晃讓他感到畏懼
崎嶇不是每個人的本意
猶豫兩岸可能的危墜
過或不過
面對鋼索架起的橋
他內心無法明確主張
自己的三心二意

定義

死亡和傷痕
在森林
不需要太多同情
它們有時肥沃土地
有時默默
讓生機順勢爬升
斷裂的肢骨
有了微嫩生綠的連結
死亡和傷痕
於是
重新自我定義

抵抗死亡

生命在一座森林
也許有聲
也許無聲
也許昂然獨立
也許攀附寄生
死亡時時都在發生
抵抗
在一座森林
經常孤單

博愛

陽光對待萬物
沒有多餘的思想
在生長擠壓
互相競爭遮閉的地方
只要出現些微隙縫
騰出少許空間
陽光的穿透
是無等差的衡量

畫像

偉大的藝術家呀
你的畫筆
造作出
一個人的表情
讓文字不得不承認
已經失去
可以作用的能力

*欣賞來自羅馬尼亞音樂家女詩人Angela Furtuna在Facebook上的畫作

意志

從根部的意志竄出
想要好好活一場
是本能最好的理由
有時依附強權
因弱小別無選擇
它堅持不出賣
自信與自尊的底線
用卑微的體質
提升伸展的高度

新世代

一條溪流要經歷多少曲折
才能回到心繫的原鄉
一根臍帶要轉折多少母性
才能繫住血肉相連的愛
我們卻不知不覺
進入一個
講究截彎取直的新世代

野溪

野溪在深山唱自己的歌
岩石高低堆疊
一路相陪
看盡所有的生機與腐敗
在森林裡走反向的路
透澈思想的雜質
野溪不牽掛終極的歸宿

激浪

海象的詭譎
從無預警的平靜升起
波波激情的衝擊
讓礁石為存在
找到刻骨銘心的意義
掀湧吧
讓碎裂不盡的濤音
宣揚
悲情中隱藏的偉岸

浪潮

海的伸展沒有盡頭
海的原始節奏
一波退後
一波高起
鳥類疲累飛行
尋找邊灘降落覓食
陪伴浪潮
在無盡沖刷的礫石上
從泡沫中獲得喘息

映

總是禁不住嚮往
小時候
熟悉的鹹味海風
小漁村的風險與幸福
也常映在腦海
喜歡在不吵雜的時候
撿拾
波平浪靜
漁舟停泊映照的倒影

蟄

如果我們的世界
還存在
溫柔的大地
人間之河的漫流
不會在幽暗中蟄伏

新綠

腐朽在森林裡
慢慢把死亡留下的形體
化成土壤裡的養分
我熟悉的家人
正逐漸走向凋零
幸虧他們為我留下
許多打包在腦海的影音
當枯葉覆蓋
心中存念的土地
總會看到
悄悄冒出的新綠

距離（二）

一支笛子
一把小提琴
生動地把我叫醒
一段友誼
一個全新的今天
跨過空間
翻越語言的藩籬
心決定
人與人之間的
距離

快閃書店

如果有一種速度
以日計算
只有180天
在忙忙碌碌的都市
隱身
不被視覺壓迫的空間
讓我的愛戀
可以在更短暫的時間
長出一雙書的心靈
自由飛翔的翅膀

一朵玫瑰

一朵玫瑰
它的出生沒人注意
一朵玫瑰
不粉不白也不紅
一朵玫瑰
找不到流浪的土地
側看支撐自我的荊棘
它不忘告訴自己
我就是天生的
一朵玫瑰

奇跡

有人等待每次的奇跡
有人等待每天的奇跡
有人等待一生的奇跡
生命盛放
生命萎謝
平靜而沒有抗拒
大地用盡新奇
為無時無刻的奇跡
無言地歡呼

星空

歲月走到盡頭
有時只剩淡淡的暮色
華麗的天空
曾經為無數短暫的過客
揮灑慰藉的彩色
夜並不忘記
為新來的一天
點起心中仰望的明燈
儘管只是黑暗世界
稀疏的閃爍

夕日剪影

夕陽在高美濕地
擁有一整片惜別的天空
沉沒在沉默中
為歡送的所有身影
浮貼驚嘆的剪影

開始

日子
從早晨一朵花的盛開
起步

愛情摩天輪

愛情有顏色嗎
紅綠白藍橘……
承諾總是刺激想像
願景難免天馬行空
愛情登上摩天輪
摩登裝飾天空
高調情牽私密夜色
拒絕聲稱自己
其實不過是一盞
巨型的走馬燈

草

有一種草在高山
有一種草在濕地
長出
叢叢我愛的寫意
我禮讚造物主
揮灑這樣的毛筆
沒有花的襯托
粗獷也纖細

一條路

一條路驚心
一條曲折的脈流

一條路淡然
一個被忽視的故事

一條路埋藏暗流
活成
一個開始
一個結束

生滅

一朵花
順性開出生命的意境
一隻鳥
呼喚一片自由的天空
一滴水
融合於廣闊的溪澗海洋
一個人
最後終究
臣服於無常的生滅

樹的遐想

一棵樹
竟然對火
懷抱愛戀的遐思
不顧一切
把自己
變成火的顏色

陪伴

一棵樹
一扇窗
一輩子的陪伴

雕像

如果有人看你
如看一尊
沒有表情的雕像
你刻意隱藏的感情
就不需迴避
你們不需在彼此的
眼睛裡停格
一尊雕像並不在乎
誰是路人甲
誰是路人乙

詩

詩的相遇
如果是心靈的沐浴
連悲傷
也變得美麗

惑眾

他深知詩的語言
有曖昧的權力
他自戀擁有
玩弄惑眾的魅力
有人看見
他的劍
沾上神經性毒液
拔出鞘
指向
違逆者的背脊

如果（二）

如果金黃的色澤
來自對於秋天的理解
死亡與重生
必然相互擁抱歌頌

智者

世界如此簡單
真正的家屋
並不捆綁
以愛為名的奴僕
他在關係中
讓無等差的陽光
照進
每扇敞開的門窗

信仰

沒落的家鄉老街
被遠走的時光拋棄
鏽蝕的門窗
一路鎖住
形貌難以辨識的記憶
唯獨
光彩依舊的廟宇
始終屹立

走向內在

如果有一天
世界只剩下黃昏的霞光
人甘心回歸成
面向地平線卑微的背影
人世間所有的語詞
將因臣服而失聲

朝顏

頑強的活著
溫柔謙卑地迎接
新鮮的一天
慶祝開花

明月之心

一輪明月的爬升
無視都市的燈光紛紛亮起
它的掛念
想必落在沉寂黑暗的地方

護

陽光和煦地照耀
清晨的一朵小白花
它被強韌的綠葉
祝福圍繞
笑靨無比開懷純真
我忍不住彎下身
聞一聞淡淡的清香
卻發現葉片下
密密護衛的
是根根
讓人流血的棘刺

舞

世界剛醒
沒有人注意
盛開的
一朵小紅花
傾折柔軟的身軀
輕聲對
緊緊纏繞的根鬚
說
讓我們一起來擁舞
跳最優雅的
生之舞姿

一條街

一條街
往昔常民
從早到晚的熱絡
沒有再回來
一條街
留下許多人的過去
身影從時間流裡消失
只剩下流傳的名字
一條街
把小鎮漁獲的豐收
從路旁的一幅畫倒出
曾經熟悉的氣息

日子

日子有時昏睡
等待天光
日子有時茫醉
等待清醒
若是無風又無雨
天空擁抱日子
迎朝曦
別晚霞
有時
相互吻別

作者簡介

　　林鷺現為笠詩社社務委員兼編輯委員、《台灣現代詩選》編選委員，世界詩人組織成員。自2005年起曾參加我國與蒙古國、古巴、智利、祕魯、突尼西亞、羅馬尼亞、墨西哥的國際詩歌交流活動，以及2015至2019年之淡水福爾摩沙國際詩歌節。

　　已出版中文詩集《星菊》(2007)、《遺忘》(2016)、《為何旅行》(2017)及漢英雙語詩集《忘秋》(2017)。

譯者簡介

　　黃暖婷，現為台灣大學政治學系博士生。

　　任職台灣經濟研究院國際事務處助理研究員期間，曾任2016年我國APEC領袖代表團成員，以及2013、2014和2015年「APEC未來之聲」青年代表團輔導員。

生滅
Life And Death

Life And Death

Spring

Set out from a little yellow flower in the wilderness

Persistently

The entangled winter wind is still in its hot pursuit

My frosted hair is still on an impulse

Perceiving that

My mother far away

  can no longer embrace

  the last

Spring

Mountain

Why you are so near the sea

With ebbs and flows

With ups and downs

You show your original color when the sky is clear

You become a piece of gray shadow when the sky is cloudy

With highs and lows

With backs and forths

You stick yourself

Into those quiet days

Sea

Outside of the windbreak
The fluctuating white sideline
Is passing the message that
The hometown is having been eroded

A huge windmill
Carefreely hanging its head---

No wind.

Under the winter sun
It only gazes
to the never ever
   aging sea

Flowers in the Morning

The pierced sparkling sunshine

Reflected

The delight of beauty

The beating tenderness

Perceived

The wildness of nature

Within a bunch of blossoming flowers

Life and death

Are lost in the flow of time

Frozen in the eternal tranquility

Frigid Winter

In the frigid winter

Obituaries come one after another

The white of snow is stained and has lost its purity

Leaves

Pedals

Are condensed in the color of blood

Dropping down

In the silent sighs

Distance (I)

So near

And so far

So clear

And so vague

I want to enlarge the image in my mind

And dwindle myself

Hiding in the warm womb again

Flowing in the breath of sea

Gift

Brewed with my whole life

Here is my best gift

No gratitude

No adoration

But a commitment from you

To hold the virtuous rose

Tightly in your heart

To love its fragrance

Implanted in your heart

Rust

Time keeps peeping

A human's rusting and corroding

Every day

As I scrutinize myself in the mirror

So have I ever contemplated

That I understand myself more than before?

My chill-sensitive knees

Begin to worry

If they can resist

The past already left way behind

Bridge

As the night dyeing the scene out of the window
So the bridge is gradually losing its figure
Only left
A sparkling chain of light
Floating in between the shores

Cross

Outside of the wall

The white fringe tree is wearing a blossoming white flowerhead

To praise the season

Without voices and words

The shining white shell bracelet

Bears the blessings from a mother's first childbirth

Tilting up my head

I praise the pure light shed from the huge cross sunroof

Which is penetrating

The labor pains in April

Rib

A rib was pulled out lusciously

From the moment

Inside this man there has been a space

That only God knows

When and how to heal and mend

He does not know

The rib he lost

Is in a human's or a wolf's mouth

Yet fortunately in his bled body

There is a fine, fine line of life

In his dim memory

Remembrance

Mother's face

Is stored

In my memories

Yet again and again

Mother's voices and shadow

Are banned from the movie theater

That I am long to get into

In every dark night

Seeing the Waterfall

A beauty in fierce

Pulling out with the extreme

Mixing up the illusion and reality

There is no time to ponder

The comes and goes of the life and death

And the sunshine

Illustrates the law of nature with shivers

A Reposed Soul

You said

Born as a Taiwanese

Ceased as a Taiwanese ghost

You said

You lived your life as a general in hardships

Tied in the lifelong battlefield

Today is a windy and rainy day

You had lived up to your true self

At the end of your commemoration

I witnessed

Your huge shadow

Has been condensed

In a small cremation urn

The Legend of Shiba-sakura

The man has gone

Yet his love still lasts

He has planted his wife's words into beauty

And his remembrance lasts to the whole green slope

Blossoming in rouge flowers

Tightly surrounding with

The legend to be said

The Waterfall of Wisteria

Shedding

Shedding

Shedding in white

Shedding in yellow

Shedding in purple

Shedding in black

The old wisteria doesn't get old

Yet augments the everlasting spring

Answer Back

Waiting for an answer
But no answer is back
Desiring to go back
But daring not to speak out
Where the home locates

Were the door open
Who would be the first in your sight
Or simply just
The breached desolation
That has already passed away

Imagination of a Fish

I am not a fish

But my birth is directly linked with

A broad and inscrutable sea

The salty sea breeze

Often reminds me

The free breath that I am longing to

Maybe once upon a time I had been a fish

Having had been swallowed at once

Has made me strive for

The free at ease that a fish should be

Denial

The cloud is light

Yet the wind is heavy

A fight over where a rose is from

Suddenly came from a distance

The rose's yellow pedals

Firmly resist to recognize

Its false birthplace

Given a poet believes in God

How dare he does not deny

An evil empire

Led by a tyranny in betrayal of God

Old

Mourn

For the days that she could no longer stand still

If the clock could counterclockwise

How sincere she would like to recycle

The long live blessings

At her birth

Desperately

She could only exchange her possible nirvana

With her last breath

Sensation in the Red Brick Building

Moistened by rain

Tamsuei enjoyed the tender embraces from the poets

Beautiful languages

Circled around the corridors of the Red Brick Building

Every line is a praise

From the hearts of various nations

Scar

No longer flawless

A thunder

Sliding with the wrong step

Left a trail

On the surface of my forehead

Given God just cannot white it out

I can only accept

Suspicions from readers

Hakka Indigo Blouses

Dyed in indigo

The Hakka blouses

Outline their women's tranquil modesty

Trimming the blouses on the front

The laces pipe out

The grandmother's advice

Married women should be modest for their vows

Yet fancy is for single ladies

To call upon

Their potential romances in springtime

A Mountain

Enough

As a mountain

Nothing blocks you at your sight

Only the sunshine brightens you

And the clouds and mists are coming to surround you

Without your permission

Being a mountain

Everyone wants to know

How you think about

Yourself

When you are alone

A Flower Vendor

Watching the busy street

Are the crowds

Distant

From your lonely heart

Your flowers are in simple colors

Yet could the cardboard box you are sitting on

Afford

All the loads of your life

If (I)

If
There is a beauty
   encountering with you in a haste
Or
   just dropping by your side
Why not let the searching eyes
Shoot with a click
To decorate
The view in memory

Red Leaves

On a tree

Escaped from seduction

The luxurious rouge leaves

Should not be requested

To restrain

Their tenderness

Window Grill

Separated yet not segregated

Acquaintance

Is still part of daily life

To let the distance

Be naturally transparent

Instead of

Being abruptly offended

Red And Blue

An innocent red leave

Wrote down

A passionate poem

In the clear blue sky

Eyes

There is a brightness

Coupled to shine as lamps

At the forest in the darkness

Please be sure to extinguish

Your desire of peeping

To ensure

Freedom and trust

Need not to flee away

Your Painting

——To a Taiwanese painter

Your mountain

Contains the hopes from our growth

Your ocean

Contains the heart sounds from our mothers' embryos

Your ship

Contains the load of the whole island

In the Pacific Ocean

Suspension Bridge

Dangles threaten him

Roughness is not people's original intention

Hesitating to the potential landslide in between the strait

To pass or not to pass

On facing the bridge in iron wires

Deep in his heart

There is no clear answer

From his half-hearted considerations

Definition

In the forest

Deaths and wounds

Do not need much sympathy

For sometimes

They fertilize the earth

And sometimes

They cultivate the living creatures

Broken branches

Are therefore connected by green sprouts

Hence

Deaths and wounds

Have been granted

In their new definitions

To Resist Death

In a forest

Perhaps

Life is sounded

Life is soundless

Life is dependent

Life is independent

Deaths happen all the time

In a forest

Resistance

Often is the forsaken case

Philanthropy

The sunshine

Treats all the creatures with no difference

In a densely crowded environment

Competitions are in a tea pot

As long as

There is a gap to hack off some space

The transparency of sunshine

Will be an indifferent evaluation

Portrait

O great artist

Your pen

Has created

A person's moods

So well expressed

That to force the words

Cannot but reluctantly

Recognize their impotence

Will

Sprouted from the root
The will want to live up to its best life
With its instinct

Sometimes
Clinging to the powers
Is due to its weakness

Although humble in nature
The will insists
Its bottom line of self-esteem and confidence
Trying to reach out to the sky high

New Generation

How many tortuous routes

Should a stream go through

To back to its dreaming hometown

How much maternity consideration

Should an umbilical cord carry out

To tie on the love between parents and children

Yet unconsciously

We have entered into

A "straightforward" new generation

A Wild Creek

A wild creek
Singing her songs in the mountains
Passing all the lives and corruptions
   through piling rocks

Filtering the impurities
   on her way backward to the forest
A wild creek does not care about
The end of her eternity

Treacherous Waves

The treacherous waves

Soar out of the blue

Their passionate crushing

Carved the reefs

Deep into their lives

Over the surges and declines

The voices of ebbs and flows

Are proclaiming

The greatness hidden in sadness

Tides And Waves

The ocean stretches beyond the vastness

Its original beats

Step back and forward

Tired seabirds

Landing on the beach for their food

Found their relief

Swirling in the tides and waves

With the small rocks and bubbles

Reflection

Can't resist my wonders

To the familiar salty sea wind

In my childhood

The risk and happiness in the small fishing village

Often reflect in my mind

In placidity

I like to pick up

The reflections of the fishing boats

  in the tranquil tides and waves

Crouch

If
The tender motherland
Still
Exists in our world
The flows on the earth
Will not
Crouch under the darkness

Sprout Green

In the forest

The bodies left behind the deaths

Are gradually corrupted and converted

Into the fertilizer of the earth

My family members

Are also fading away gradually

Yet they have already packed up

Their voices and pictures

Deep in my mind

When the leaves cover up

The land deep in my mind

I can always see

The green sprouts

Budding on the quiet

Distance (II)

A flute

A violin

Wake me up vividly

A friendship

A whole new today

Crossing the space

Crossing the barriers of languages

It is the heart

To decide

The distance in between

Flash Bookstore

If there is a speed

Measured in days

It is hidden in a city in haste

　for just 180 days

A vast space

　not limited in the short sights

Has shortly incubated my love and affection

　into a pair of wings

To fly freely

　with the spirit of books

A Rose

A rose

There no one cares about her birth

A rose

Neither pink nor white not even red

A rose

That she cannot root on her wonderland

With a squint

She looks at her supporting thorns

Telling herself

I

Am a rose

Miracle

Some people wait for miracles in times

Some people wait for miracles in days

Some people wait for the miracles in their lives

There are lives blossoming

There are lives withering away

Calm acceptance without resistance

The land uses its mystery to the extreme

To cheer in silence

For the miracles at all times

Starry Sky

Sometimes

The end of the seasons

Is only the dusk going opaque

The spectacular sky

Once comforted with colors

For numerous passersby

Yet the night doesn't forget

To light up the torches in hearts

Despite

They are only the sparse stars

In the vast darkness

The Silhouette under the Sunset

In the Gaomei wetland
The sunset
  bears a whole sky bidding farewell
Sunk in silence
The sunset
  attached on the amazing silhouettes
To reply
  those who are bidding farewell

Commencement

A day

Set out

From a flower's blossom

In the morning

The Love Ferris Wheel

Does love have color?

Red, green, white, blue, and orange....

Promises always stimulate imaginations

Visions cannot avoid going crazy

When the love climbs up to the Ferris wheel

Modernity decorates the sky

And the affair also climbs up to the cloud nine

Yet the Ferris wheel

  refused to admit

It is only a huge

Trotting horse lamp

Weeds

In the mountains
At the wetlands
The clumps of grass
Sketched my consciousness

I praise the Lord
For his magnificent strokes
Without the foil of flowers
The wild weeds
Are tamed in elegance

A Route

Thrill

Brought all the comes and goes around

Placidity

Perceived an ignored story

Within the hidden undercurrents

A route

Lives up to

A beginning

And

An end

Life And Death

A flower
Blossoms the nature of life
At her will

A bird
Calls out a free sky
With her twitters

A drop of water
Converges into
The vastness of rivers and oceans

A human
Finally surrenders
To the uncertainty of life and death

The Reverie of A Tree

How dare

A tree

Could have

The reverie of affection

To the fire

Till burning itself

To the color of fire

Accompany

A tree

A window

A lifelong accompany

Statue

If someone looks at you

As looking at

A statue with poker face

The emotions you are hiding

Have lost their purpose of circumvention

You do not need to stop

In each other's eyes

A statue does not care

Who are the passersby

Poetry

If
The encounter of poems
Is the bath of spirits
Even the sadness
Can convert into
Beauty

Allure

Deeply he understands

The language of poems

Bears the power of flirting

Which brings out his narcissism

From misleading others

Someone saw that

His sword

Has dipped into the neurotic poison

Ready to extend from the scabbard

Pointing onto

The spines of the mavericks

If (II)

If the golden color

Comes from the understanding of autumn

Then death and resurrection

Must embrace and praise

Each other

Wiser

The world is simple

A real home

Does not bind the slave

In the name of love

In the relationship

The sunshine

Trespasses all the opening windows

With indifference

Belief

The declining old street in my hometown
Has been abandoned by the time walked away
Rusted windows and doors
Locked the dim memories all the way
All but the spectacular temple with its brightness
Stand still as its way

Back to Inward

If one day

In the world only the twilight is left

People are therefore willing to convert

Into the humble shadows facing the horizon

All the words in the world

Would lost their sounds because of surrender

Morning Glory

Living out with a tough stance
Yet welcoming a whole new day
With meek and humble blossoms

The Heart of A Bright Moon

Regardless of the lights in a city lightened gradually

A bright moon climbed up to the sky

Supposedly

Its missing has lost

In the insignificant darkness

Escort

A small white flower
Bathed under the balmy sunshine
Surrounded by the blessings
From tenacious green leaves
Shed from its heart
Was its innocent beams

Attracted by its incomparable purity
I bent down
To sniff at its light fragrance
Yet I found that
Escorted under its green leaves
Were its bleeding thorns

Dance

The world just woke up

No one pays attention to

A blossoming

Little red flower

Bending on her soft body

Whispering to the bounded vines

Saying that

Let's embrace and dance

Dance

In the most graceful

Life steps

A Street

A street

Lost its crowds from day to night

Where the left civilians

Are no longer back

A street

Reserved many people's past

Where their shadows have been lost in time

Yet their names are left in words of mouth

A street

Where the fishing harvest of a small village

  with the familiar smell

Is poured down by a picture on the street

Days

Sometimes

Waiting for the daybreak in lethargy

Sometimes

Waiting for the soberness in drunk

If the weather is neither windy nor rainy

The sky embraces days

To welcome the dawn

To bid farewell to the dusk

And sometimes

The days and nights

Kiss and say goodbye

About the Author

LIN Lu (b.1955) concurrently serves at the standing committee of the Li Poetry Society, the editorial board of the Li Poetry Magazine, and the jury of annual Taiwan Modern Poetry Collection. She is a member of Movimiento Poetas del Mundo (PPdM). As a poet actively participating in international poetry festivals, she attended several international poetry festivals held in Mongolia, Cuba, Chile, Peru, Tunisia, Romania, and Mexico since 2005, as well as the annual Formosa International Poetry Festival in Taiwan from 2015 to 2019.

LIN Lu's publications in Mandarin are Star Chrysanthemum (2007), Lost in Time (2016), and For What to Travel (2017). Her Mandarin-English poetry collection is Forgetting Autumn (2017).

About the Translator

Faustina Nuanting Huang is a doctoral student in the department of political science at the National Taiwan University.

During her years serving as an assistant research fellow at the Chinese Taipei APEC Study Center and the Chinese Taipei Pacific Economic Cooperation Committee, she was a member of the Chinese Taipei APEC Leader's Delegation in 2016, as well as the educator of Chinese Taipei APEC Voices of the Future Delegation in 2013, 2014, and 2015.

CONTENTS

語言文學類　PG2413　台灣詩叢11

生滅 Life And Death
——林鷺漢英雙語詩集

作　　　者／林　鷺（Lin Lu）
譯　　　者／黃暖婷（Faustina Nuanting Huang）
叢書策劃／李魁賢（Lee Kuei-shien）
責任編輯／林昕平、石書豪
圖文排版／周妤靜
封面設計／蔡瑋筠

發 行 人／宋政坤
法律顧問／毛國樑　律師
出版發行／秀威資訊科技股份有限公司
　　　　　114台北市內湖區瑞光路76巷65號1樓
　　　　　電話：+886-2-2796-3638　傳真：+886-2-2796-1377
　　　　　http://www.showwe.com.tw
劃撥帳號／19563868　戶名：秀威資訊科技股份有限公司
　　　　　讀者服務信箱：service@showwe.com.tw
展售門市／國家書店（松江門市）
　　　　　104台北市中山區松江路209號1樓
　　　　　電話：+886-2-2518-0207　傳真：+886-2-2518-0778
網路訂購／秀威網路書店：https://store.showwe.tw
　　　　　國家網路書店：https://www.govbooks.com.tw

2020年8月　BOD一版
定價：220元
版權所有　翻印必究
本書如有缺頁、破損或裝訂錯誤，請寄回更換

國家圖書館出版品預行編目

生滅：林鷺漢英雙語詩集 / 林鷺著. 黃暖婷譯
-- 一版. -- 臺北市：秀威資訊科技, 2020.08
　　面；　公分. -- (語言文學類)(台灣詩叢；11)
中英對照
BOD版
ISBN 978-986-326-818-5(平裝)

863.51　　　　　　　　　　　　　109006685

讀 者 回 函 卡

感謝您購買本書，為提升服務品質，請填妥以下資料，將讀者回函卡直接寄
回或傳真本公司，收到您的寶貴意見後，我們會收藏記錄及檢討，謝謝！
如您需要了解本公司最新出版書目、購書優惠或企劃活動，歡迎您上網查詢
或下載相關資料：http:// www.showwe.com.tw

您購買的書名：＿＿＿＿＿＿＿＿＿＿＿＿＿＿＿＿＿＿＿＿＿＿＿＿＿

出生日期：＿＿＿＿＿年＿＿＿＿＿月＿＿＿＿＿日

學歷：□高中 (含) 以下　　　□大專　　　□研究所 (含) 以上

職業：□製造業　□金融業　□資訊業　□軍警　□傳播業　□自由業

　　　□服務業　□公務員　□教職　　□學生　□家管　　□其它＿＿＿

購書地點：□網路書店　□實體書店　□書展　□郵購　□贈閱　□其他

您從何得知本書的消息？

　　□網路書店　□實體書店　□網路搜尋　□電子報　□書訊　□雜誌

　　□傳播媒體　□親友推薦　□網站推薦　□部落格　□其他＿＿＿＿＿

您對本書的評價：(請填代號　1.非常滿意　2.滿意　3.尚可　4.再改進)

　　封面設計＿＿＿　版面編排＿＿＿　內容＿＿＿　文／譯筆＿＿＿　價格＿＿＿

讀完書後您覺得：

　　□很有收穫　□有收穫　□收穫不多　□沒收穫

對我們的建議：＿＿＿＿＿＿＿＿＿＿＿＿＿＿＿＿＿＿＿＿＿＿＿＿

＿＿＿＿＿＿＿＿＿＿＿＿＿＿＿＿＿＿＿＿＿＿＿＿＿＿＿＿＿＿＿＿

＿＿＿＿＿＿＿＿＿＿＿＿＿＿＿＿＿＿＿＿＿＿＿＿＿＿＿＿＿＿＿＿

＿＿＿＿＿＿＿＿＿＿＿＿＿＿＿＿＿＿＿＿＿＿＿＿＿＿＿＿＿＿＿＿

11466
台北市內湖區瑞光路 76 巷 65 號 1 樓

秀威資訊科技股份有限公司　　　收
　　　　　　　　BOD 數位出版事業部

....

（請沿線對折寄回，謝謝！）

姓　　名：＿＿＿＿＿＿＿＿　年齡：＿＿＿＿　性別：□女　□男

郵遞區號：□□□□□

地　　址：＿＿＿＿＿＿＿＿＿＿＿＿＿＿＿＿＿＿＿

聯絡電話：(日) ＿＿＿＿＿＿＿＿　(夜) ＿＿＿＿＿＿＿＿＿

E-mail：＿＿＿＿＿＿＿＿＿＿＿＿＿＿＿＿＿＿＿